To my four children,
DANTE, CHRISTA, CHASE, and CHARIS.
*You are dearly loved and **beautifully crowned.***
—Dorena

To my nieces,
XHAYDAH, XHENNA, KYRIE, and KYLA,
and all the beautiful young girls
who continually inspire me to illustrate pictures
in which they can see themselves.
—Shellene

CROWNED WITH GLORY

Text copyright © 2022 by Dorena Williamson
Illustrations copyright © 2022 by Shellene Rodney
All rights reserved.

Published in the United States by WaterBrook, an imprint of Random House,
a division of Penguin Random House LLC.

WATERBROOK® and its deer colophon are registered trademarks
of Penguin Random House LLC.

ISBN 978-0-593-23440-2
Ebook ISBN 978-0-593-23441-9

The Library of Congress catalog record is available at
https://lccn.loc.gov/2021000460.

Printed in China

waterbrookmultnomah.com

10 9 8 7 6 5 4 3 2 1

First Edition

Book and cover design by Jessie Kaye
Cover art and interior illustrations by Shellene Rodney

SPECIAL SALES Most WaterBrook books are available at special quantity discounts
when purchased in bulk by corporations, organizations, and special-interest groups. Custom
imprinting or excerpting can also be done to fit special needs. For information, please email
specialmarketscms@penguinrandomhouse.com.

CROWNED WITH Glory

written by
Dorena Williamson

WATERBROOK

illustrated by
Shellene Rodney

Hello, world! I'm a gift from above.
I already know that I am loved.

Gazing around with a **great big grin**—
there's a whole wide world for me to take in.

Little legs struggle to sit for a while
as Mama twists a **curly style.**

Turning the pages, what do I see?

Visions of **color, happy** and **carefree.**

Rain, rain, don't go away!

I'll just pull on a
hood so I can play!

Am I as pretty as the girls I see?

I'm an original—**free to be me!**

LEAP, BEND, ARABESQUE.

I gracefully move my arms and legs.

Braided tightly so I can stroke—
extra conditioning keeps my **plaits dope.**

Sporting a **topknot** with a bit of flair
so I can jump without a care.

Sitting still as hours go by.
Look in the mirror—

girl, you so fly!

Bantu knots or twist-out fun,
a beauty puff in a **textured bun.**

Reflections of culture all around—
such glory in creating beautiful **crowns.**

At night I put on my **protective cap** to take care of my hair and keep it **wrapped.**

A dab of gel so my edges **stay put**
for days on end, making me look good.

Headed to church with my pretty hair bow—
worship and the **Word** help my faith grow.
Learn to pray and bow my head,
thanking **God** for my daily bread.

So **excited** on picture day,

wearing my hair a **special** way.

Curious hands.
"Can I touch, pretty please?"
So many questions I could charge a fee!

I'm worthy of **honor** and much **respect,**

so if you wanna learn,
better **come correct!**

The Creator crowned me with melanated glory, and every day I get to live out my beautiful story.

Using that **passion** that God gave me to make a difference in my community.

Working through tangles
one by one—

it always feels good
when hard work is
done.

I'm confident and **one of a kind.**

I won't let anyone dim my **shine!**

Imagine all the **possibilities**—where I can go and what I can be!

Rock my natural, keep my focus **strong**—
this **sharp mind** has a lot going on.

Graduate, and off to college I'll go and find new styles to keep **my glow.**

No glass ceiling will stand in my way—
I will **persist,** come what may.

Got a great big cheering squad of family, full of **wisdom** and **love,** always ready for me.

In my circle of support are my best friends,
faithful and loving through **thick** and **thin**.

I'm full of **hope** from head to toe.

There's no limit to the places I can go!

Plans before me—just walk them out,

a future full of seeds to sprout.

Goodness and mercy follow all my days,
and this **crown of beauty** will never fade.